Louise's Gift

by Irene Smalls

Illustrated by Colin Bootman

Little, Brown and Company
Boston New York Toronto London

Louise's Gift

or What Did She Give Me That For?

Also by Irene Smalls:
Irene and the Big, Fine Nickel
Jonathan and His Mommy
Dawn and the Round To-it
Irene Jennie and the Christmas Masquerade
Father's Day Blues
Ebony Sea
The Alphabet Witch

For my great uncle Johnny and my great uncle Clarence,
who help teach me.
"I love you, black child."

I. S.

To Shantaquira Brendera Johnson

C. B.

First Edition

Library of Congress Cataloging-in-Publication Data

Smalls-Hector, Irene.
    Louise's gift / by Irene Smalls ; illustrated by Colin Bootman. — 1st ed.
        p. cm.
    Summary: Louise is disappointed in Nana's gift and prediction for her
future, but later comes to understand just how special she is.
    ISBN 0-316-79877-0
    [1. Afro-Americans — Fiction. 2. Family life — Fiction. 3. Self-acceptance —
Fiction.] I. Bootman, Colin, ill. II. Title.
PZ7.S63915Lo 1996
[E] — dc20   94-34504

10 9 8 7 6 5 4 3 2 1

NIL

Published simultaneously in Canada by Little, Brown & Company (Canada)
Limited and in Great Britain by Little, Brown and Company (UK) Limited

Printed in Italy

Louise was excited. Today her new baby cousin, Kevin, was being presented at a party to Nana, the eldest, for formal welcome into the family. Best of all, today each child was getting a gift.

Harlem, New York, where Louise lived, was a place of kinship corners. An aunt lived here, an uncle there. Every corner provided kinship and love. All the family elders were coming: Great Aunt Merle, Great Uncle Clarence, Great Uncle Johnny....They were taking this special day off from their jobs as cooks, maids, and janitors for the celebration.

As the guests came in, the party began.

The last to arrive was Nana. Nana was deep black with naturally red hair. She had brought her magic shopping bag. It was just a plain brown paper bag, really, but Louise knew of its wonders. Out of the magic shopping bag came apple pies and an asafetida healing bag. Later the special gifts would appear.

Once Nana had settled in her chair, Kevin's mother placed him in her arms.

"See that lap baby," Aunt Myrtle chortled as Kevin was passed from lap to lap.

After Kevin had been presented, Louise and all the other children lined up to be given their special gift and saying. The elders were so wise they could look into a child's eyes: view their souls and the future.

Each year Nana went into her magic shopping bag and came up with wonderful gifts. This year for Cheryl, it was a bright shiny penny. "You'll be rich in gold and in the spirit," Nana said.

For Hazel, it was a small comb. "Pretty you will be, but pretty you must act," Nana advised.

For Eric it was a ruler. "You will be tall, strong, and stand out in many ways," she told him.

For Dawn, it was a secondhand book. "Gain wisdom from books and your heart," Nana instructed.

For Jimmy, it was a joke from a bubble gum wrapper. "You have the gift of laughter. Your laughter will bring great joy," she declared. The magic shopping bag seemed to have no end to its wonders.

Then it came time for Louise. She could see that the shopping bag was nearly empty. It had ceased to bulge and looked limp and tired like an old balloon. But Louise was still excited. The other gifts were so marvelous. Louise knew that her gift would be just as special. Nana looked into Louise's eyes and said, "I give you the gift of a blank page on which you can put whatever you wish." Out of the magic shopping bag came a small rumpled piece of paper.

Louise couldn't believe it. "Is that all I get?" she mumbled. "An old raggedy piece of paper." She stared at the floor. Hearing her, her mother whispered, "Yo momma ain't birth no fools in this world. Say thanks."

"Uh, she don't know what she's talkin' about," Louise's mother continued nervously, giving Louise a look that could freeze hot coffee.

But Louise kept on speaking: "I want to be the prettiest or the smartest or the richest. Why give me the tiniest gift? What can I do with that?"

Louise's mother raised her right hand to the heavens. It was unheard of to complain about one's gift from the elders. No child had ever done that before.

"Oooooh," Hazel, the youngest, said.

"Chile has gumption," Great Aunt Merle quipped. "Must be from her father's side."

All of the other kids were fiercely looking at their shoes.

"Funny baby cry with milk in her mouth," Great Uncle Johnny stated with a shake of his head to Great Uncle Clarence.

But Nana just started to chuckle, and when she laughed, it was so free that her feet, her arms, her whole body laughed with her. "Chile, if you don't understand it, just keep on living," Nana said between fits of laughter.

Louise was still sad, but her mother's pointed looks had finally found their mark. "Thank you, Nana," Louise said cheerlessly. "Thank you."

All the other kids went out to play. The grown-ups went back to cooing at Kevin.

Louise mumbled to herself, "My gift isn't special. And I'm not special. I want to be the prettiest, the strongest, the richest, the funniest. What am I? A blank piece of paper! Uhh. Some gift — it's no use. No use at all."

Louise was miserable. She was not going out to play with nobody nowhere. She went into the kitchen and sat in the corner on the floor by herself.

Nana came in the kitchen to get another cup of tea and saw Louise. With some effort, she got on her knees so they could look each other in the eyes. Nana always looked children in the eyes when she had something important to say.

"Let me be your bridge over troubled water. What'sa matter, chile?" she asked.

Louise started to cry. "My gift is no use," she bawled.

"Chile, your gift is the sum of all those others but greater," Nana offered. "Go on out and play. Go along, now, I say."

Louise didn't dare to act up in front of an elder again, so, reluctantly, she joined the other kids outside in the park.

The kids were climbing the rocks to the top of the world.

"Last one to make it to the top is a rotten egg!" Jimmy yelled.

Louise was scrambling up the rocks when Hazel started to whimper.

"What's the matter with the baby?" Louise taunted.

"I dropped the ring from the Cracker Jack box. I can't get it!" Hazel wailed.

Eric moaned. "Momma told us not to touch that ring after we fought over it."

Dawn, who often acted like Miss Smartie Pants, said, "Losing something your mother told you not to touch is worse than two doses of castor oil on Saturday night or being sick on your birthday. We better find it quick!"

Cheryl, who was to be the richest, just scratched her head. Eric, who was to be the strongest, pushed and puffed but couldn't move the rock. Jimmy, who was the funniest, couldn't even make a joke about this mess. And Hazel, the prettiest, had lost the ring in the first place.

But Louise had an idea, something she'd seen in the back of a comic book. "Get that piece of board," she said to Eric. "Slip it under that rock. Now, push."

Eric pushed, and the ring popped out.

"I saved you but good," Louise sniffed at Hazel.

"Some truck is stuck under the bridge," Dawn said. She ran over to get a closer look. "They got people and big machines coming from downtown to try and get it out."

Everybody poured out of the building to watch the commotion. "All the fancy people from downtown coming uptown," Great Aunt Merle remarked.

The adults from the neighborhood laughed behind open hands at the fancy folks. They enjoyed seeing the people from downtown sweating for a change.

The driver of the truck tried to back up and then he tried to go forward, but the truck didn't budge. The big machines pushed and pulled, but the truck stayed stuck right where it was.

"That ol' truck looks like a giant can of pork and beans with the top being pried off." Jimmy laughed, and everyone around him laughed, too.

"This is boring," Louise said after a while.

As she got up to leave, Louise thought of something. She ran up to the man with the fanciest hat, the fanciest coat, and the fanciest shoes. "Mister, take the air out of the tires!" Louise shouted.

At first, he looked at Louise as if she were crazy, but then he began to grin. "Take the air out of the tires," he yelled. His work crew let the air out of the tires. *Whoosh, whoosh, whoosh, whoosh,* the air sang as it slipped out.

The truck moved.

Everybody cheered. Louise's face bubbled a smile.

Nana came off the stoop. "You did good, chile," she said. "I have a fancy word for you to put on that piece of paper. Cre-a-ti-vi-ty. You are creative."

"Nana is right," Louise shouted. "I have a very special gift. I'm creative."

EASY Dup card 08984
SMA

AUTHOR
SMALLS-HECTOR, IRENE
TITLE
LOUISE'S GIFT, OR
WHAT DID SHE GIVE ME
THAT FOR?

DATE DUE	BORROWER'S NAME	ROOM NUMBER
4/8/14	1-02	
11/4	2-02	
10/24	Victoria Verna	

E
SMA

Smalls-Hector,
Irene.

Louise's gift, or,
What did she give me
that for?